M000301308

For my little cappuccinos and cioccolatini:
Noah, Milo, Zen and Lotus
and for Paola and Filippo at Elle Effe Restaurant in Rome

www.theenglishschoolhouse.com

Copyright 2021 © by The English Schoolhouse

All rights reserved. This book or any portion thereof may not
be reproduced or used in any manner whatsoever without
the express written permission of the author except for
the use of brief quotations in a book review. This is a work
of fiction. Names, characters, places, and incidents are a
product of the author's imagination. Any resemblance to
actual persons, events, or locales is entirely coincidental.

ISBN: 978-1-955130-18-9

# OGNI RICCIO UN CAPRICCIO

## A Book of Italian Proverbs

By Dr. Tamara Pizzoli

Illustrated by Riccardo Gola

# MEGLIO UN UOVO OGGI CHE UNA GALLINA DOMANI.

## BETTER TO HAVE AN EGG TODAY THAN A HEN TOMORROW.

QUANDO IL GATTO NON C'È
I TOPI BALLANO.

WHEN THE CAT'S AWAY,
THE MICE DANCE.

IL LUPO PERDE IL PELO
MA NON IL VIZIO.

A WOLF LOSES IT'S FUR,
NOT ITS VICE.

IL BUONGIORNO
SI VEDE DAL MATTINO.

A GOOD DAY STARTS
IN THE MORNING.

# NON È TUTTO ORO
# QUELLO CHE LUCCICA.

# ALL THAT GLITTERS ISN'T GOLD.

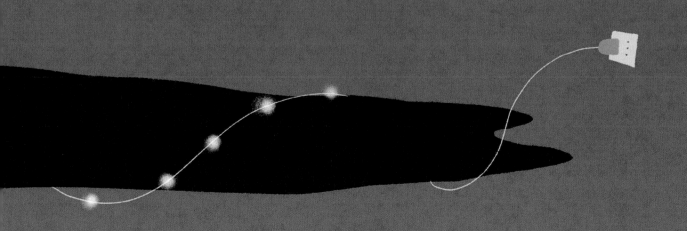

**UNA MELA AL GIORNO
TOGLIE IL MEDICO DI TORNO.**

**AN APPLE A DAY
KEEPS THE DOCTOR AWAY.**

# CHI NASCE TONDO

## THOSE WHO ARE BORN ROUND

**NON MUORE QUADRATO.**

**CANNOT DIE SQUARE.**

# RIDE BENE
## CHI RIDE ULTIMO.

## THE ONE WHO LAUGHS LAST
## LAUGHS THE BEST.

# CAN CHE ABBAIA
# NON MORDE.

# A DOG THAT BARKS
# DOESN'T BITE.

CHI HA I DENTI NON HA IL PANE.
THOSE WHO HAVE TEETH HAVE NO BREAD.

**CHI DORME
NON PIGLIA PESCI.**

**THOSE WHO SLEEP
CATCH NO FISH.**

# L'ERBA DEL VICINO

## THE NEIGHBOR'S GRASS

# MEGLIO SOLO
## BETTER TO BE ALONE

IF YOU'VE ENJOYED THIS BOOK,
CHECK OUT THESE OTHER STORIES BY

# THE ENGLISH SCHOOL HOUSE

AVAILABLE FOR PURCHASE AT
THEENGLISHSCHOOLHOUSE.COM
OR ON AMAZON

OR SCAN ME!

**TALLULAH**
THE TOOTH FAIRY CEO

Dr. Tamara Pizzoli · Pictures by Federico Fabiani

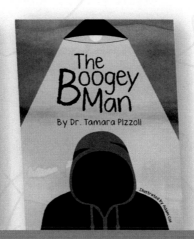

The
Boogey
B Man

By Dr. Tamara Pizzoli

Illustrated by Komi Con

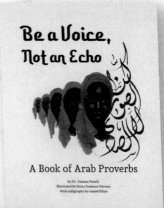

Be a Voice,
Not an Echo

A Book of Arab Proverbs

By Dr. Tamara Pizzoli
Illustrated by Elena Tommasi Ferroni
With calligraphy by Amjed Rifaie

**GENEVIEVE
AND THE GIANT**

BY DR. TAMARA PIZZOLI · ILLUSTRATED BY ELENA TOMMASI FERRONI

**TWELVE ABYSSINIAN
PRINCESSES**

By Dr. Tamara Pizzoli · Illustrated by Elena Tommasi Ferroni

**FIRST DAY OF
FIRST GRADE**

By Dr. Tamara Pizzoli

Illustrated By
Eleonora Jacomo

**Books are for More
than Just Reading**

By Dr. Tamara Pizzoli & Ben Burchall
Art by Seneca